W9-AEO-152

Three Cheers for Hippo!

John Stadler

Thomas Y. Crowell New York

Three Cheers for Hippo!

Printed in the United States of America. For information address Thomas Y. Crowell Junior Books, 10 East 53rd Street, New York, N.Y. 10022. Published simultaneously in Canada by Fitzhenry & Whiteside Limited, Toronto.
10 9 8 7 6 5 4 3 2 1

First Edition

Library of Congress Cataloging-in-Publication Data
Stadler, John.
Three cheers for Hippo!

Summary: Hippo cleverly comes up with a plan to save Cat, Pig, and Dog just when it looks as if they are about to parachute into a swamp full of alligators.
[1. Animals—Fiction] I. Title.
PZ7.S77575Th 1987 [E] 87-497
ISBN 0-690-04668-5
ISBN 0-690-04670-7 (lib. bdg.)

To my pals, Kaitlin and Lauren Bonenberger

Hippo is here.

Cat speaks.

Hippo holds Cat's hand.

Hippo flies the plane.

Pig and Dog are happy.

Cat is scared.

They jump.

Cat wants help.

Hippo is near.

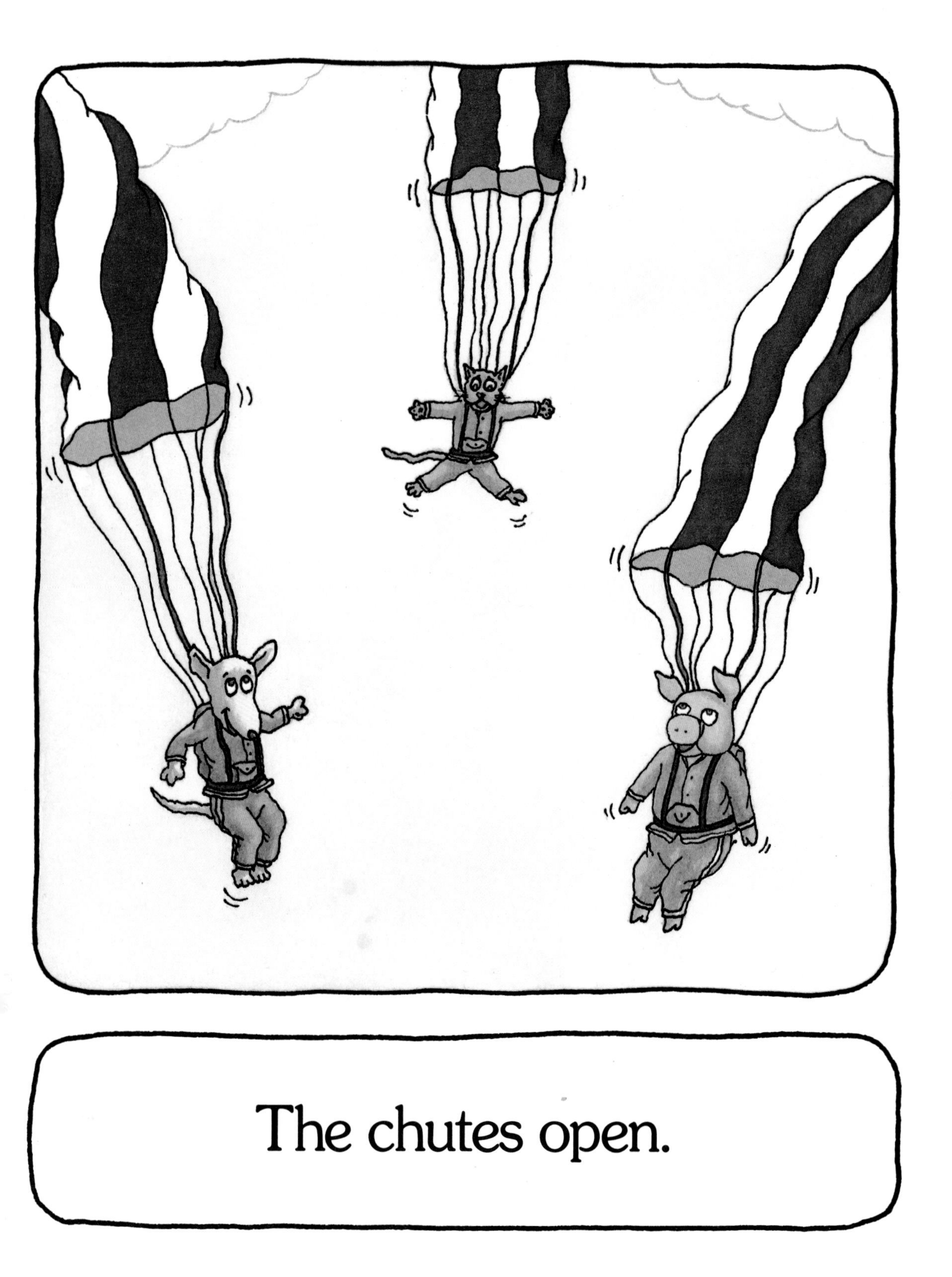

The chutes open.

They float down.

Cat has fun.

The swamp is below.

Cat wonders.

Gators!

Cat is upset.

The gators look up.

Hippo flies by.

The gators wait.

They are nervous.

There are many gators.

They worry.

The table is set.

They want Hippo.

The gators open wide.

The table shakes.

Hippo rises.

The gators run away.

Three cheers for Hippo!
Hippo is here.